Paul McCartney's

RUPERT
and the
FROG SONG

adapted by David Hately

Ladybird Books

RUPERT and the FROG SONG

Rupert Bear woke up one morning feeling in just the mood for an adventure.

So after breakfast he asked his mother if he could spend the day in the hills. Mrs Bear wasn't very sure at first, but in the end she agreed.

"Now, remember to keep well wrapped up," she said, tying Rupert's scarf round his neck. "We don't want you to catch a cold, do we?"

Rupert promised, and said goodbye to her. As he shut the kitchen door behind him, he murmured happily, "Off to the hills!"

He said cheerio to his father, who was already hard at work in the garden, and ran to the gate leading out into the lane.

Rupert liked to share adventures with his friends, so he was pleased to see Edward Trunk and Bill Badger turning the corner of the lane. Bill was pushing a pram.

"I'm going for a walk in the hills," said Rupert. "Want to come?"

"I wish I could," said Edward Trunk, "but I have to do some shopping."

"And I have to look after my baby brother," sighed Bill.

Rupert peered into the pram. Baby Badger gurgled at him, and gave a little hiccup.

"What a pity!" said Rupert.

So Edward and Bill set out for the village, while Rupert headed for the hills.

Rupert was sad that his friends couldn't come with him. But by the time he got to the top of the first hill he was happy again, so he did a handstand and stood on his head to celebrate!

At the top of the next hill he was out of breath. He sat down under a tree to have a rest.

The leaves of the tree were brightly coloured, and Rupert sat back to look up at them.

Suddenly they started to shudder, then to flutter, and Rupert realised that they weren't leaves at all! They were butterflies!

The butterflies swarmed round Rupert's head, then swooped off towards a clump of rocks.

"I wonder why they flew over there," Rupert said to himself and, full of curiosity, he walked towards the rocks to have a look.

If Rupert had looked behind him, he would have seen a wicked-looking barn owl settle on a branch of the tree, and two snarling cats creep behind its twisted trunk.

They were hunters, out on the prowl.

They watched Rupert with interest, and wondered if he had found something that they could pounce on.

Their eyes glittered.

When Rupert reached the clump of rocks, most of the butterflies had gone. So instead of butterfly spotting, the little bear decided to do some rock climbing.

Then he heard a noise from the ledge above his head.

"Brekkety-brek. Brekkety-brek."

Whatever the noise was, it wasn't butterflies.

When Rupert pulled himself up above the rocks, he found the ledge packed with frogs!

And what amazing frogs they were! Some were green, others were blue. There were yellow ones and red ones, too.

The frogs were so surprised to see Rupert that they leaped away, croaking anxiously as they jumped to safety.

High up among the rocks, the wicked barn owl looked down and smiled a cruel smile.

He liked nothing better than a big meal of frogs' legs.

His eyes glowed red in the shadow of the rocks as he watched Rupert begin to follow the frogs.

Rupert hurried along a rocky path that led to a stream.

As he stood there, dozens of frogs began jumping from a high rock into the water below. *Plop!* they went as they hit the water. *Plop!*

All the frogs began to swim upstream towards a waterfall. One frog, who had never quite got the hang of swimming, paddled away furiously in an old tin mug, using wooden spoons instead of oars. He made worried little frog noises as he went.

Rupert wondered what all the fuss was about. The waterfall looked just like any other.

And then he saw that the water fell over the rock like a curtain. And the curtain hid a huge split in the rock.

Rupert was excited. He pushed his way behind the waterfall. He had found a secret cavern!

Inside the cavern it was dark and eerie. When Rupert's eyes became used to the gloom he saw a large sign saying: FROGS ONLY BEYOND THIS POINT. Below it was another that read: EVERYTHING EXCEPT FROGS MUST BE KEPT ON A LEAD. A third notice said: GUARD FROGS OPERATING.

As Rupert tiptoed into the cavern he saw several giant bullfrogs on guard! Luckily, the frogs didn't spot him, so he tiptoed on.

Soon Rupert had reached a clearing, part underground and part open air. When he looked up he saw the stars twinkling as they do on a frosty night.

Rupert was puzzled. The sun had been shining when he crept behind the waterfall. So why were the stars out now?

"Perhaps I'm in a magic land!" he thought to himself.

Rupert hid behind a large fern and looked around.

In the gloom he could just make out a music stand on a rock platform. Suddenly an important-looking green frog hopped onto the rock.

The frog raised a little stick and gave it a flick in the air. Instantly, a lantern made of fireflies sprang into light!

Now Rupert saw that the huge cavern was packed tight with frogs of every shape, size and colour. There were frogs as far as the eye could see.

They all leaned forward eagerly as soon as the green frog appeared. Rupert could tell that something was going to happen.

But what? He hadn't the slightest idea!

Sitting quite close to Rupert's hiding place
was a frog wearing a smart cloth cap. With
him was his son, a junior frog, scarcely more
than a tadpole.

Junior squirmed. "Dad! Dad!" he said in a
loud whisper. "Eh! Dad! When's the show
going to start then, Dad?"

The frog in the
cloth cap hissed,
"Now listen, son!
This only happens
once every two
hundred years! If
you don't pipe
down I'll...
I won't bring you
again!"

Junior thought that his dad was going to clip him, so he held up a little webbed foot, just in case, and yelped, "Oich!"

All the frogs sitting nearby began tittering. His father blushed, and smiled.

But Rupert had learned what he wanted to know.

This was an important assembly! It only happened every two hundred years!

There was going to be a show!

All at once an orchestra began to tune up. One or two latecomers hopped about anxiously, trying to find their seats.

The green frog was flipping through some music, looking for the right page. Then, after a moment of dead silence, he tapped twice on the music stand, and hummed a couple of tuneful croaks to give the right note: *"Croak, croak."*

And the Frog Show began.

It started with a chorus of bullfrogs in bow-ties who had deep, deep voices. Rupert supposed that they were bass-bullfrogs. Then the tenor frogs sang the melody, and soon everyone was swaying in time to the music.

Rupert was spellbound.

He especially liked the trio of dainty young lady frogs, all dressed in blue, who sang in harmony as they twirled round a rock pool on a scallop shell.

The song they were all singing said something about, "*Win or lose, sink or swim,*" something...something...something, "*We all stand together.*"

All the frogs looked happy and loving as they sang. Even the frog in the cloth cap was smiling fondly at his son.

The show was very romantic.

Two young frogs kissed tenderly after a ballet sequence, when an elegant male frog with green tights leaped about with a willowy female frog in a frothy skirt.

Then a goldfish joined in. He sang in a very grand way, standing on his tail in the middle of the pond.

At last the goldfish was dragged back underwater, screaming, by two little fish who decided that the frogs could do without him.

Nobody noticed that the wicked barn owl and the two snarling cats had found their way into the secret chamber.

They looked greedily at the fat little frogs.

Soon Rupert was nodding his head in time to the music. "*Play the game*," he heard them sing. "*We all stand together.*"

There was also a lot of "*ba-ba-ba, ba-ba-ba,*" and a good deal of "*la-la-la, la-la-la.*"

But the wonderful show hadn't finished yet! There was an air ballet, danced by special guest stars, the fireflies and will-o'-the-wisps.

Some athletic frogs put on an underwater ballet, their bodies making strange shapes and shadows beneath the pool's surface.

Then there was a display of synchronised swimming by a team of smiling young frogettes, and Rupert was enchanted when hundreds of hot air balloons arrived. Each balloon was guided by a frog pilot in goggles.

"Surely it must end soon?" thought Rupert.

Suddenly the waters of the pool began to stir. They seethed. They boiled. Then they exploded into a pillar of water right in the middle of the pool.

And as the waters cleared away, Rupert at last understood why all the frogs of the world had gathered in assembly. For there, standing on a water lily blossom, wearing crowns and holding sceptres, were the two most royal frogs it was possible to imagine.

There was no doubt about it! Here were the Frog King and Queen. Their subjects had gathered to pay loyal homage. Rupert could scarcely believe his eyes!

Neither could the barn owl.

The King and Queen were the two biggest, tastiest looking frogs he had ever seen.

He had to have them!

As the song ended, the Frog King and Queen struck a noble pose. There was a moment of silence, then the audience broke into wild applause.

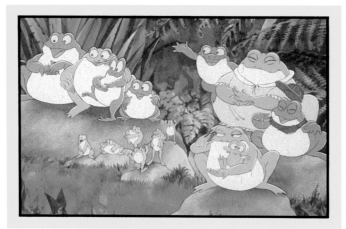

The cloth capped frog and his son went mad with cheering.
Even the goldfish reappeared, and for the first time in his life was applauding somebody else.

As the exhausted conductor took a special bow, the King and Queen smiled upon him.

And then the barn owl swooped.

At first Rupert thought it was part of the show. Then he realised that the barn owl was going to attack the Frog King and Queen.

Rupert had to do something!

"Look out!" he cried in a high, clear voice.

The King and Queen looked stunned, but they moved quickly.

One moment they were standing on the lily flower. The next they had dived underwater.

They were not a moment too soon. The sharp talons of the barn owl stretched out for them, but all he got was a bit of the water lily petal.

All the other frogs were saved, too, for they had time to jump into the big, deep pool.

The cavern was empty!

Rupert wondered if he had been dreaming. But when he looked up he saw the outline of the barn owl as the bird flew across the moon. And high on the rocks were the shadows of the two black cats slinking away.

As Rupert stood there lost in thought, a voice began to echo around the cavern.

"Roo-pert!" it called. *"Roo-pert!"*

The voice brought Rupert back to his senses. His mother was calling him! If he were late back he wouldn't be allowed to spend a day in the hills ever again!

So Rupert rushed home as fast as his legs would carry him. As he ran he tried to sing the song he had heard. *"Da-da-da, da-da-da... we all stand together."*

"They're never going to believe this," he said to himself. "Wait till I tell Edward Trunk and Bill Badger what they've missed! FROGS ONLY BEYOND THIS POINT! Ha!"

And Rupert chuckled as he ran.

Soon Rupert caught sight of his mother standing patiently by the garden gate.

"Mum!" he shouted. "Mum! You should have seen what I saw!"

"Yes, dear!" she murmured.

"There was a frog show in an underground cave," called Rupert breathlessly. "And an owl swooped down and I shouted 'Look out!' and... and... all the frogs were swimming and dancing and singing..."

"Yes, dear! Oh, that's nice," said his mother.

Rupert was still talking as he and his mother walked up the garden path and into the house.

"It was a wonderful show... butterflies... frogs near a waterfall... *Plop!*... really it all happened... really it did!"

"Yes, dear!" his mother murmured as she closed the door.

All through supper Rupert talked and talked
about his great adventure in the hills, and that
night he lay awake for a long time thinking
about the wonders he
had seen. The tune
of the Frog Song
was going round
and round in his
head... round
and round.

Afterwards,
Rupert could never
say for certain whether
the words that came to
him were the words that
the frogs had sung, or whether
he made some of them up himself to fit the tune.

But it is true that Rupert knew
the Frog Song by heart before he
fell asleep. And these were the
words he sang:

"WE ALL STAND TOGETHER."

1.3. Win or lose, sink or swim,
2. Play the game, fight the fight,

one thing is cer - tain we'll ne - ver give in. 1. Side by
but what's the point on a beau - ti - ful night. 2.3. Arm in

To Coda

side,   hand   in   hand,}
arm,   hand   in   hand,}   we all   stand____ to-

ge - ther.____   Ba   ba ba   ba ba ba

Ba   ba   ba   ba ba ba ba   ba.   La_____

British Library Cataloguing in Publication Data

Hately, David
    Paul McCartney's Rupert and the frog song.
    I. Title
    823'.914[J]   PZ7
    ISBN 0-7214-1028-6

First edition

Published by Ladybird Books Ltd Loughborough Leicestershire UK
Ladybird Books Inc Lewiston Maine 04240 USA

Printed in England